CAPE Approach

A Compassionate Method to Christian Counseling, Crisis Hotlines, and Soul Care

By

Judith A. Justiniano-Houts

ISBN: 0-7596-7585-6

Library of Congress Control Number: 2002102671

This book is printed on acid free paper.

Printed in the United States of America
Bloomington, IN.

1stBooks – rev. 3/1/02

Content

Dedication

To my husband, Joel A. Houts, a man of compassion and true love, a man of prayer and of action. He has always listened to me with an empathic ear and a compassionate heart. He knows how to laugh and cry with me.

To the survivors of the attack of terrorism in Lower Manhattan, New York, and Washington, DC; and to everyone who has or will work with the people who have been emotionally affected by this terrible act of terrorism.

Preface

This book grows out of my deep concern for people behind the bars of painful memories of the past, out of compassion for the brokenhearted, and deep understanding for survivors of abuse.

As a survivor of abuse, former lay worker, crisis hotline volunteer, pastor and now a pastoral counselor with a doctoral degree in Theocentric Counseling, I saw the need for a simple God-centered model to help counselors, pastors, caregivers, and lay workers help free others of painful memories. I also saw a need to help counselors and others in the helping profession help themselves. So many times pastors, lay people and counselors have no one to minister to them, but are expected to continue giving and producing positive results.

The stories in this book are true. However, to maintain confidentiality, names have been changed. I've used examples from churches and Christian agencies I either worked for attended to help illustrate my point.

On many occasions, I use the word counselor to refer to all people involved in the helping profession or helping ministries such as Help Hotlines or church lay counseling. All Bible references are from the New King James Version, unless otherwise indicated.

The approach outlined in this book is very simple in definition but powerful in outcome. It is a Godly approach taken directly from Jesus' example when He walked the earth.

I know that God's Spirit will move in the midst of those who sincerely and prayerfully use this model in an effort to help their clients become what God created them to be.

Chapter 1

Introduction

Christian counselors, pastoral counselors, lay counselors, and other Christians in the helping profession struggle with a similar question, what is the best Christian approach (model) to Christian counseling? There are so many to choose from in the secular world. The Christian world also offers several approaches, making the decision even harder for those of us who help people.

In the Christian arena, we find the Strategic Pastoral Counseling Approach. In my opinion, it is limited in its ability to assist the pastor decide the length of the counseling treatment and it requires the helping professional to be active and directive with his approach. Another known approach is the Nouthetic Approach, by

Jay E. Adams (1970). This approach is a confrontational one. It requires that the ill clients accept that they are sinners. Adams says about his approach,

> Sometimes when counselees are cornered and forced to acknowledge that their behavior is irresponsible, they attempt to dodge the issue by replying: "Well, I guess that's just the way I am." They say this in a resigned manner and expect to leave the whole matter right there (p. 74).

Although confrontation sometimes is necessary with some clients, and only on some occasions, I don't think it is the best Christian approach to counseling. The fact that they are sitting in an office in front of a counselor should tell us that they do not want to leave the matter there, they want to be healed. What many of these clients need is love and understanding, not more controlling personalities in their lives, not more accusations of being immoral or a bad person. What they need is the touch of a caring Christian counselor that will assure them that through Christ everything will be all right.

Like any other counselor, the Christian counselor should develop his or her own style and use an approach that is going to help clients develop better psychologically, emotionally and spiritually. This decision should not be taken lightly and should be done under fervent prayer. Collins (1991) says the following about the Christian counselor's duty, "The Christian counselor has a mission to serve Christ as a people-helper and burden bearer who brings psychological and spiritual healing, even if there is criticism from secular counselors or from fellow believers" (p. 17).

Helping people to eliminate self-defeating behavior and make correct choices in order for them to become what God created them to be is not easy, but it is the calling of the Christian counselor. It can only be done with the guidance of the Holy Spirit and by following Jesus' example.

Christian counselors not only need the guidance of the Holy Spirit but they also need the gift of discernment. Discernment is needed in order to detect any spirits of darkness either oppressing or possessing the client. I believe that Jesus left us plenty of examples for every situation we will encounter in the helping profession today. He was the Founder and Executive Director of the first Ministry of Compassion ever established in this world. He had a staff of twelve and many volunteers.

It is interesting to note that most, if not all, of His volunteers were people healed through His ministry. Some of them were Mary Magdalene, Lazarus, Zacchaeus, and Matthew the tax collector. To me this means that these people believed in Jesus' method and wanted to join Jesus in helping others. I call Jesus' approach the CAPE Approach (Christ- Like Model). This is the approach I recommend for all Christians in the helping profession. No matter the personal style, if the CAPE Approach is followed, the counselor cannot go wrong and God will always be glorified.

The rest of this book will deal with how to use this Godly approach, given to me by the Holy Spirit Himself. In the Agape Haus Association, Inc. Battle Creek, Michigan (1987-1997), every time this approach was used, the result was a 100% success rate. Any time I, or any member of the staff or volunteer worked in the flesh, the results were disappointment and frustration, not only for us but also sometimes for the client. I don't think that the success rate was pleasing to God.

I remember Ruth Ann (name changed for protection of the client). She came to our support group looking for a place of refuge and healing for her past sexual abuse and neglect from her parents. I was very compassionate at first. I had the best plan, so I thought; until things did not go the way I had planned. I knew Ruth Ann needed inner healing, healing from her past, and healing of her memories. She needed to forgive herself, release forgiveness to her perpetrator and forgive her parents for not loving her and believing in her. Ruth Ann needed a lot of love, but she had never known Agape love and could not understand it. I had planned to introduce her to the Great Healer and to introduce her to His unselfish love, to His healing touch, the good touch. Not the touch she had come to know and dislike and that had driven her to a mental hospital.

Ruth Ann was progressing fast and the results were outstanding. Then I had an emergency leave. I did not leave the group under a Christian caregiver while I was out; instead I stopped the meetings. She made friends with people who although good, needed help too. In my opinion, they were not the best persons to befriend her at the moment. She was still weak and her faith was smaller than a mustard seed. I requested of Ruth Ann that she not spend so much time with her new friend, but she insisted and got very irritated with me. I lost my compassion and then demanded she stop seeing them if she wanted our services. Ruth Ann chose her friends and stopped her intervention. I don't believe she received complete healing, neither spiritual nor emotional. I lost my compassion, Ruth Ann lost trust in me, and I disappointed Jesus.

I run into Ruth Ann every now and then and, oh, how it hurts me to have lost compassion at a time of crisis. We talk. She is stuck where we left off and has chosen to remain there. It is true that it is more than she ever had, but it was not all God had intended for her to have. God has forgiven me and so has Ruth Ann, but it was a hard and painful lesson to learn.

God loves His children and His desire is that they have peace and abundant life. Lack of inner peace is what brings instability to people's minds and emotions. But because the counselor does not know at what stage of life the person was robbed of inner peace, he or she needs to have a Christ-Like Approach to reach into that part of the individual's life and teach him how to allow the Holy Spirit to begin the inner healing. For some people, the healing is instant; for others, it is a very long process. God is the healer and He can take all the time He wants. We, the counselors, are His helping hands; it is our duty to use the best instruments available for us today.

The greatest thing about the CAPE Approach is that it can be used by empathic listeners in prayer or Help Hotline volunteers, by pastors helping parishioners in their spiritual walk, and by counselors and clinicians in short or long term clinical counseling. The method is simple enough that parents, teachers, and caregivers can use it, yet it is deep enough that psychologists, clinicians, counselors, and psychiatrists can use it too.

May God help you as you launch yourself into using a compassioned approach used by Jesus Himself in His personal ministry on the earth 2,000 years ago.

Chapter 2

What is The CAPE Approach?

CAPE is an acronym for **Compassion, Action, Prayer, and Empathy**. Compassion without action is as faith without works. The Apostle Paul says in James 2:17 "...faith by itself, if it's not accompanied by action, is dead." To understand this statement let's discuss verses 15 and 16 of the same chapter. They read, "Suppose a brother or sister is without clothes and daily food. If one of you says to him, 'Go, I wish you well; keep warm and well fed,' but does nothing about his physical needs, what good is it?"

In other words, if a person tells a brother in need that his faith in God will solve his problem and does not get personally involved in the solution, the helper is displaying both lack of faith and a dead spirit. This kind of talk is a Christian cliché and a way out of a Christian responsibility. It is not faith! It's an excuse for not doing what God asks us to do; it's a way of getting personal attention, recognition and inflating one's own ego. It's a way of spreading false hope. It's not only not Christian-like, but selfish.

The same situation is true with a helping professional. If a person comes with a crisis to a counselor and the counselor does not identify herself with the emotional problem the individual is experiencing, then she has no compassion. She might be in the helping field for personal and selfish reasons. Here is what Kottler (1993) says about this issue.

Becoming a therapist is one way some people seek to fulfill their need for power and control.

Others are attracted to the opportunities for having successful relationships with minimum personal involvement.

Still others who feel stupid can act wise, those who are selfish can pretend to be altruistic, and people who are timid can be assertive (p. 209).

True compassion only comes from God. True compassion was born in the Garden of Eden when God went to visit Adam and Eve and found out that they were scared and were hiding from Him. He understood their emotional situation, "had compassion," and immediately went into action. He made garments of animal skin and clothed them. This is the first example of compassion and action. The example came from God Himself. Later, while on the earth, His Son gave us many more examples of compassion, some of which we will discuss as we discuss the CAPE Approach.

The CAPE Approach should be seen as a warm coat used during a cold winter day, a raincoat used during a rainy day, a shawl used during a cold spring morning, and sometimes an umbrella to protect a person from the rain.

Your compassion, empathy, action, and intensity of prayer have a lot to do with the issues at hand and the personality of your client. All of the above mentioned garments are used to protect an individual from different types of weather. The same is true with the CAPE Approach. See it as a spiritual cape, coat, umbrella, raincoat or shawl that you are symbolically using to protect your client from the weather of his emotions as both of you work together to reach an emotional climate that is comfortable for him or her.

Protecting The Clients From The Weather of Their Emotions

As a coat keeps a person warm during a cold winter day, the CAPE Approach can warm the soul.

As a raincoat keeps a person dry during a rainy day, the CAPE Approach can help the spirit of a grieving person.

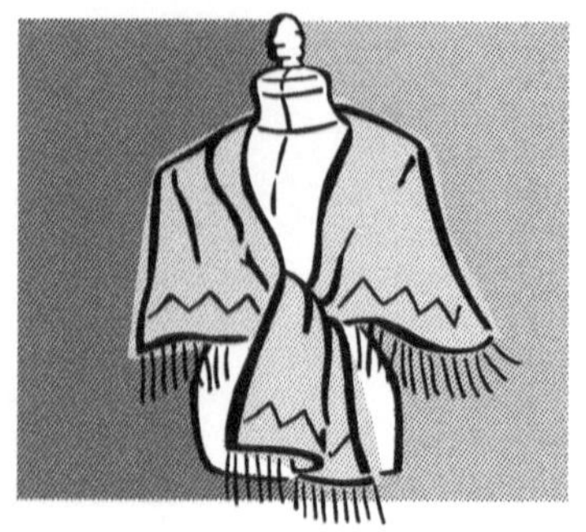

As a shawl brings warmth during a cold spring morning, the CAPE Approach can bring comfort to an empty nester.

As an umbrella protects a person from the rain, the CAPE Approach can protect an individual from unhealthy shame and guilt.

The four Phases of the CAPE Approach

Phase I, Compassion

Compassion must not be confused with sympathy. Sympathy is feeling sorry for the individual. It's putting yourself higher than the person with the crisis. Compassion is the understanding and identifying with the client's problem or pain. Compassion is what Jesus felt for the people to whom He ministered during His earthly ministry. He saw and understood the pain and fear in Mary Magdalene's eyes (Luke 8:2), the sorrow and grief in the widow's body as she walked next to her son's coffin (Luke 7:12-15), the hunger in the multitude's faces (Matthew 14:16), and the pain of rejection in the little children's eyes (Matthew 19:13-14).

He understood the paralytic's frustration as he lay next to the pool of Bethesda waiting for someone to put him in the water when the angel moved it (John 5:6) and understood Mary and Martha's pain when their brother Lazarus died (Luke 11:14).

Jesus understood the bride and groom's embarrassment when they ran out of wine during the wedding celebration (John 2:3,8) and He also understood His mother's pain, agony, and loneliness when He was dying on the cross (John 19:26-27). Jesus understood compassion and wants us to understand it, too. He was a compassionate person and wants us to be one also. Mathew 9:36 says, "But when He saw the multitudes, He was moved with compassion for them, because they were weary and scattered, like sheep having no shepherd."

When a client seeks the help of a counselor, she is doing it because she is weary and because at times her thoughts and feelings are scattered.

She has comes to you because she, too, needs a shepherd to help her find the answers to unanswered questions, the reason for her pain, and a way out of her past. We as Christian counselors should be moved with compassion and into action immediately, without hesitation, just as Jesus was moved.

There are many ways of showing compassion to your client. Among them are paying close attention to what they are saying and asking questions, either to understand them better or to clarify a statement. Repeating back to them what they told you will eliminate putting words into their mouths. Plus, they will see and hear that you are listening to them. Listening correctly is not only a form of communication; it's a way of being compassionate.

Compassion will show in your face; your facial expressions will give you away. The way you look or react to what the client is telling you will let her know if you are accepting her or being judgmental. Compassion includes giving your client your undivided attention. If your attention is absorbed by something else, such as being late for your next appointment or problems with your children at home, it is better to be sincere with the client and tell her you missed what she was saying, and can she please repeat herself?

If you know ahead of time that you will not be compassionate because of your own personal problems, then it is better that you reschedule or ask someone else to see the person for you on this occasion.

If you just cannot be compassionate because your client's problem is hitting home, then the client and you are better off if she is referred out and you take time to deal with your own problem. It is time for someone to show compassion towards you.

We all need compassion; our problems seem less heavy when we have someone who gives us compassion and an empathic ear.

I'm reminded of Jesus before His betrayal. He went to

Gethsemane with three of His disciples to pray and to talk

to God the Father about His ordeal. He left the disciples in

a place quite close to Him; I want to believe. He wanted

them close, but not too close! It was that night above of all

nights He needed His friends. He needed compassion.

Jesus went to pray. He cried out to His Father about

His fate. He even asked if it was possible that He achieve

what He came to earth to achieve without having to go

through the death in the cross. Then He thought about it

again and in His agony he just told the Father to do what

He had to do and not to mind His request. This means that because He was going through a life-changing event, He was not able to think too clearly and He was just trying to get someone to be compassionate to Him. Jesus was in distress, He was in a crisis, and He needed someone to listen to Him.

Jesus finished His prayer, perhaps He cut it short like we do sometimes when we are under a lot of stress, and walked over to His disciples; they were asleep. They were unconcerned. They took Him for granted. They had no compassion for their Master. It is here when He said, "Could you men not keep watch with me for one hour?" (Matthew 26:40, NIV Study Bible)

I believe Jesus was saying, "Couldn't you wait up for me so that we could talk about what I'm going through?" Or perhaps, "I've listened to you so many times, and now that I need you, you are not there for me." Maybe He was also telling them, "Treat others like you would like to be treated." In summary, Jesus needed people of compassion on the night of His betrayal and found none. In the same manner, many people are looking for compassionate caregivers. Are you willing to be one?

I remember Pastor Ken. He was a man of compassion. I remember when I first attended his church, how interested he was in me, and my children's well being. As I told him about my financial problems due to my recent separation from my husband, tears ran down his face. I did not know what to make of it. Either he was in pain and I was taking up his time or he had problems of his own and mine were overwhelming him. But no, he was "For Real!"

A year after my emotional turning point, I was doing better and was ready to get a job, but I had no car and no money for a down payment. Pastor Ken was my co-signer for a brand new car that we happened to find at a great price. He did this out of compassion. I'm not saying that you now have to run and buy cars for all your clients that need one, nor am I saying to cry with your clients. I am saying that compassion has many ways of manifesting itself and if you are truly a compassionate person, it will show somehow and your client will notice.

One of the biggest benefits of compassion is that it will create an environment where your client will trust you easier. No clinician is able to be productive and successful in this profession unless his clients trust him. What better way to build trust than to be compassionate?

What are some external and internal forces that can adulterate compassion?

These can be biases, racism, prejudice, lust, hatred, un-forgiveness, a wounded heart, loneliness, lack of self-esteem, frustration, hurts, ignorance, and a lack of relationship with God to mention some.

It is important that the caregiver be aware of these barriers to compassion and either resolve them or keep them in check while he is working with the client.

Phase II, Action

Compassion puts the helping professional in a position to take action. The question every helping professional should ask is, "Now that I understand what my client is going through, what am I going to do to help her with the problem?" Sometimes, the only immediate action the counselor or helper can take is being there, providing a listening and compassionate ear, as often happens in crisis Help Hotlines.

For example, in a crisis Help Hotline, if the caller is coming across as not capable of taking the agreed upon steps in coping with the situation, or seems to be suicidal, then the helper devotes her energy in helping save the caller's life. Some actions can be calling a family member for the caller, calling an outreach team to visit the home, or sending a rescue unit to the home of the caller. Slaikeu

(1990) refers to this emotional state of the caller as high lethality.

On the other hand, if the helper judges low lethality in the caller's voice, the helper's action must be focused in talking the caller through the problem and offering emotional support in conjunction with an offer of outside help, such as referral for counseling.

The actions to be taken by a counselor when providing face to face counseling are similar to the steps previously described. For example, the counselor assists the client in establishing goals, making right decisions to achieve the goals, and helps her follow through with actions so that the goals established can be accomplished and healing received. In the worst-case scenario, the counselor convinces the client to commit herself to a mental health hospital. These are only examples of actions that can be taken to preserve someone's life. Of course, every staff member and volunteer need to be informed of their agency's guidelines and policies.

We all know that the Help Hotline volunteer's action is limited but very important. He or she should be under the supervision of a trained and licensed counselor, social worker or psychologist if working in a community setting and by professional trained staff if working in a faith based organization.

In other words, the Action Phase refers to actions taken for and with the client to help her or him cope with the situation and help her or him develop to a new full potential. I say new potential because perhaps their potential was never discovered or because they might never go back to being who they fully were; maybe better or perhaps different, but all together good.

Sometimes the action can include homework such as reading assignments or writing a daily journal. Other times the action includes the counselor looking up some support group names, phone numbers and addresses and writing them down for the client. Yet other times, it might include making the first phone call for the client and doing follow-up to ensure that the client is attending meetings agreed upon and is doing well. The Action Phase also includes the diagnosis and the treatment selected for the client in the case of a licensed counselor or psychologist.

In summary, the Action Phase can be as simple as a prayer performed by the Help Hotline volunteer or lay person or as complicated as the counselor calling the mental health hospital and arranging for the client to be hospitalized immediately. The counselor should always keep in mind the words of Slaike (1990) that "individuals are still responsible for what they think, feel, and do" (p. 61). The counselor is only responsible to help his client go through the present unorganized stage into a growing stage, with the cooperation of the client himself. These two Phases cannot be taken lightly and must be done while operating in Phase III, the Prayer Phase.

Phase III, Prayer Phase

Prayer is the best way to communicate with God. Therefore, before going into action, the counselor must pray. All actions should be decided under fervent prayer. Our guidance comes from above. God is the Great healer. The Holy Spirit is the Great Counselor and Helper. It is because of heavenly guidance that we can undertake an action full of compassion.

The counselor must ask for guidance from the Holy Spirit either in an audible or silent prayer, but I repeat, no action should be taken without divine guidance. The Word says in 1 Thessalonians 5:17, "Pray without ceasing." Therefore, the Christian counselor must be in constant prayer, audible or mental, throughout the day. All Christian workers and volunteers in the helping profession need to practice what I saw written in a church sign in Etna Township, Ohio. It read, "Arm yourself with prayer."

Jesus tells us in the Bible that anything we ask from the Father in His name we shall receive. He also commands us to seek and to knock. He said that if we seek we will find and if we knock the door will be opened. This means that the Spirit is ready to give us direction in which way we should go, either for giving a diagnosis, choosing a treatment, or assigning homework. He will open our intellect and will allow us to find the correct words of encouragement, therapy, or referral. He will guide us to a true diagnosis because He is a Spirit of Truth.

A Christian counselor who does not pray requesting Holy guidance is like a soldier in a war without the proper equipment. He will be at a great disadvantage with his enemies and eventually is going to get hurt or killed. His ignorance and lack of preparation can cause emotional scars and perhaps the lives of his comrades.

The same is true with a Christian counselor doing counseling in the flesh. He or she is leaving doors open for Satan to come in and confuse the situation. This can cause long term negative effects on the client as well as in the counselor's spiritual life which can have an adverse effect on his or her ability to do future Christian counseling as well as on his or her own spiritual growth.

A Christian counselor needs to be bold in the Lord and obedient to the voice of the Holy Spirit. I remember once when a lady came in for soul-care. She was very suicidal. She was pacing and speaking very fast. She was fidgeting and had hand tremors. I had never been exposed to this type of client. I knew that a negative power greater than her and me was in action. I silently prayed for the Holy Spirit's guidance.

I was instructed by the Holy Spirit to pray over her and to tell her that this was a demonic spirit that wanted to kill her (a spirit of suicide) and that I needed her permission to cast it out. She agreed and that's exactly what I did. It was amazing how her entire persona changed. I saw a silhouette of a man-like figure leaving her. He left the room out the window as I commanded him to do. Immediately peace came upon her. Her distorted face was immediately restored and she accepted Christ as her Savior. She later confessed that she had made up her mind that my agency was the last one she was going to visit and that if, after talking to me, she did not see a way out of her depression and misery she was going to commit suicide.

If I had not obeyed, I would have been trapped in a spirit of fear and failure and surely she either would have committed suicide or been sent back to a Mental Health hospital. It was an unforgettable experience to see God's peace take hold of this lady. This brings to memory a poem Susan E. Fair found in a church bulletin (undated). It reads:

Peace is not a place,

someone once said;

it is not a destination

to be sought out

or somehow earned or won.

Instead,

peace is a way of living.

It is found in the extra-ordinary moments

of an ordinary life...

the contagious laughter

only a child creates,

the comforting touch

from a trusted friend's hand,

and the tender joy

that comes from

knowing the Creator of Peace Himself.

Peace...

May I embrace it today on my journey,

and may I welcome the Prince of Peace

into my heart.

(Author unknown, reprinted by Susan E. Fair)

This poem clearly describes the new person my client became. This poem can help the counselors explain peace to their clients and perhaps make it part of their treatment goal. This is real peace, the peace that only Jesus can give. This peace is at our disposition for the asking, or should I say for the "praying".

In my unpublished training manual for Christian Help Hotline volunteers, I have a chapter on "Three-Way Communication." I explain how the empathic listener listens to the caller, talks and listens to the Holy Spirit, and talks to the caller at the same time. I continue saying that in almost every occasion the caller is doing the same thing; talking, listening and talking to the Holy Spirit, and receiving a spoken communication from the empathic listener. In the CAPE Approach the three-way communication is slightly different. Instead of the client talking to God and to you and listening from God, it is the counselor that is talking to the client and at the same time silently asking God for guidance and God responding with answers to her petitions. In other words, in time of crisis, the client will see the counselor as the people of Israel saw the prophets in the old times. A good example is found in Judges 4: 4-5: It reads:

Now Deborah, a prophetess, the wife of Lapidoth, was judging Israel at that time. And She would sit under the palm tree of Deborah between Ramah and Bethel in the mountains of Ephraim. And the children of Israel came up to her for judgment.

Clients will come to you for help, many times to request that you speak to God for them. This is true in cases when the person is a Christian who has lost his joy of salvation because of the emotional trauma he is experiencing. There are always exceptions to the rules. There are times that some clients do communicate with God as they talk with the caregiver. In most cases they do it in small talks such as, "God help me, heal me, or help my counselor help me."

Figure 2.1 will help explain my point on the CAPE Approach three-way communication. The client talks to the counselor, the counselor talks to the client and to God. God talks to the counselor and sends His peace and insight (on His time) to the client.

Figure 2.1

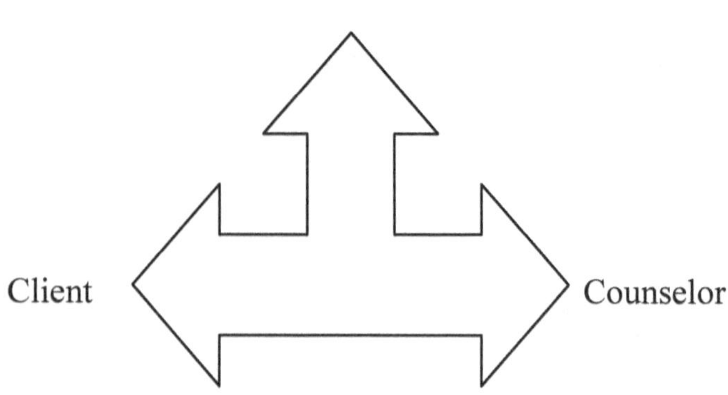

On September 2001, in the morning and on my way to the Ministry, I was listening to the Christian radio station WCVO located in New Albany, Ohio. I heard a radio-evangelist/teacher encouraging her radio audience to bring their bitterness to the cross. She assured them that if they did that, they would have a good weekend. To a point she is correct, anyone is welcome to bring his or her problems to the cross. Nevertheless, some people need help. They are so overwhelmed with pain and suffering that they can't even get out of bed, much less carry burdens to the cross. This is where a compassionate caregiver takes action in prayer. This action is very Biblical, the Spirit of God says through the apostle Paul in Galatians 6:2, "Carry each other's burdens..." (NIV Study Bible). I truly believe the apostle is not saying to the believer to carry the other person's burdens to their own home, to their families, nor to the church's congregation, but to the cross of Jesus Christ.

While editing this book, the New York Trade Center and the Pentagon in Washington, DC were horribly attacked by terrorists (September 11, 2001). They hijacked four planes and later crashed three of them into these buildings. Thousands are missing and are believed to be dead. A fourth plane crashed in a field in Pennsylvania. It was believed it was on its way to Camp David, Maryland, a place of retreat for the President of the United States, or on its way to the White House, the President's residence.

Because of this tragedy there are a lot of people hurting due to the death of family members, co-workers, or friends, and because of the destruction of their identity. There are a lot of *burdens* to be carried to the cross of Jesus in the days to come here in America. The point is that some of these people cannot carry the burdens on their own; they will be counting on hotline volunteers, pastors, priests, and professional caregivers to help them carry their heavy burdens and broken hearts to the cross of Jesus. Yes, they can have a good weekend, but only through the joy of the Lord, the empathic ears, faithful prayers, and compassionate actions of Godly caregivers.

Phase IV, Empathy Phase

According to the Webster's Dictionary, New Revised and Expanded Edition, empathy is "Understanding the feelings of another person." The Webster's New World Dictionary defines it as "Intellectual or emotional identification with another." So when a counselor understands the feelings of a client in crisis or identifies with his or her emotions, then and only then the counselor is being empathic, thus entering the fourth Phase of the Cape Model.

Empathy is a learned behavior. Romans 3:12c says, "There is none who does good, no, not one." On the other hand, we are instructed to repent from sin and do good. Therefore, if empathy is a good thing and there is not even one who does good, then we must repent from our apathy and lack of compassion and learn empathy. This is accomplished through studying and practicing appropriate listening skills and techniques, by humbling ourselves to the Lord and by learning to carry each other's burdens, as the Lord indicates in Galatians 6:2.

Understanding the pain of a client is as if you were walking in her shoes. By walking in someone else's shoes you know if they are tight, comfortable, clean, dirty, smelly, fashionable or just plain old and raggedy. By understanding your client's pain and crisis, you are walking her path. You can see and sometimes feel her pain, shame, and guilt. By understanding her pain, unhealthy shame, and guilt, you will be better equipped to work with her to change the situation. David Keirsey and Marilyn Bates (1984) explain empathy when they wrote the following:

> I may be your spouse, your parent, your offspring, your friend, or your colleague. If you

will allow me any of my own wants, or emotions, or beliefs, or actions, then you open yourself, so that some day these ways of mine might not seem so wrong, and might finally appear to you as right – for me. To put up with me is the first step to understanding me. Not that you embrace my ways as right for you, but that you are no longer irritated or disappointed with me for my seeming waywardness. And in understanding me you might come to prize my differences from you, and, far from seeking to change me, preserve and ever nurture those differences (p. 1).

I believe that it is empathy that allows the counselor to share some of his experiences (self-disclosure) with the client. Empathy builds trust.

If we look closely at the words *empathic* and *empathetic*, we will notice that both words end with the letter "c". In my view they stand for *compassion* in time of *crisis*. Therefore, when the Christian counselor has reached Phase IV of the CAPE Model, he will go back to compassion. As we can see, this model is meant to lovingly wrap around the client and bring warmth and comfort. Those of us in the helping profession know that the client does not walk in to our office with just one problem. She might talk about one thing in particular, but we know that as we talk with her, one issue leads to another and that one to another. It is through our compassion and empathy, and the use of our learned techniques and theories that we are able to help the client open up and tell us her life story. It is here that the counselor needs to stay in the circle of compassion, action, prayer and empathy (See Figure 2.2). It is here where the CAPE Approach is needed and will do the job. The individual style of counseling, the techniques or the theorist you model after is only going to be enhanced by the use of the CAPE Approach.

Figure 2.2

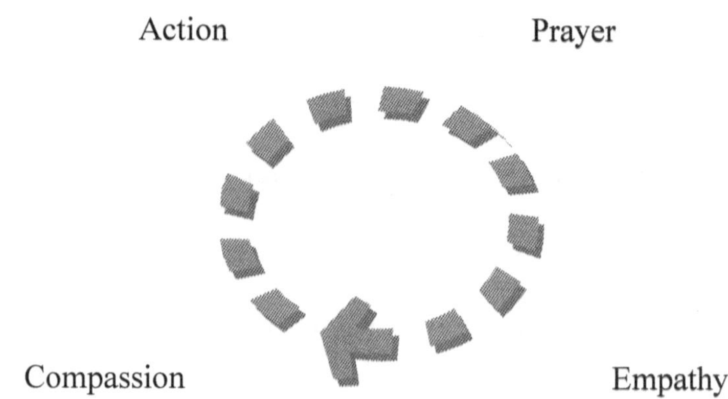

Figure 2.2 shows that the circle of the CAPE Approach is not closed completely nor it is united by one bold line. On the contrary it has openings, meaning that the counselor or helper can go from one Phase to the other as necessary in order to stay connected with the client and to ensure that the client is being served and "caped" correctly,

We've all learned in First Aid training that in order to prevent a victim of an accident from going into shock the person is to be kept warm, preferably with a blanket. This too is true for victims of emotional crises. The CAPE

Approach is simple enough that it can be used by the first

adult that comes to the scene of an emotional crisis such as

a parent, teacher, caregiver, or priest, as well as by a

counselor when the client visits his or her office.

52

Chapter 3

When to Use The CAPE Approach

It is crucial that the counselor understands that some clients will not allow them to use the CAPE Approach. They don't want to be loved and they don't want to be prayed for. One reason why some clients won't accept the love that compassion brings is because they have never been loved, nor understood. This approach is completely new to them. Patience is a virtue, and this is where the clinician has a chance to either apply that virtue or pray for it.

The client, on the other hand, might not accept prayer, because either they are not believers of Christ or they have never been exposed to it. If this is the case, there is no law against the clinician saying a silent prayer on behalf of his client and for guidance on the action he must take. There will be times when the client will refuse the Agape love. Jesus experienced this situation when the people of Jerusalem refused his help. In Matthew 23:37-38 we find Jesus reminiscing after he had offered them Compassion, Action, Prayers and Empathy, but they did not want His help.

Oh Jerusalem, Jerusalem, you who kill the prophets and stone those sent to you, how often I have longed to gather your children together, as a hen gathers her chicks under her wings, but you were not willing. Look your house is left to you desolate.

Jesus was talking here about murderers, abusers, and perpetrators. He said, "That kill the prophets and stone those sent to you" (Matthew 23:37). Jesus was looking into the future and saw the stoning of Stephen and the death awaiting His disciples. Oh, how did He want these people to come to Him for counseling! He was willing to CAPE them with His compassion and love. Some of the citizens of Jerusalem had come to Him for one reason or another. Some, I believe came seeking help for their soul and wounded heart; they just did not accept the "treatment plan" Jesus had for them. We all know about the "Rich Young Man." He came to the Lord with his greed, selfishness, and pride, but rejected help. I believe Jesus' prayer over Jerusalem included this young man.

The metaphor of "wings" here is a symbol of protection, warmth, security, love, compassion and understanding. Jesus wanted to help them, wanted to cape them with His cape of compassion, love and understanding, but they refused.

Those of us that have experienced country living know that when chicks are in danger, or when evening comes they take refuge under the hen's wings. They feel secure there. The extended wings of the hen symbolize a cape. When the chicks come to the hen for help, she "capes" them. The hen is in control and knows exactly what to do to help her young ones be safe.

The same thing happens when the clinician or counselor offers the CAPE Approach to a client in crisis. The client learns to trust the counselor and opens up. The client begins sharing intimate things from the past and the present and begins doing what his counselor asks him to do in order to get healed. The counselor that is using the CAPE

Approach will never take advantage of the vulnerability of his client. The Approach is too positive and Christ-like, leaving no room for negativity or betrayal.

One of the benefits of the CAPE Approach is that the counselor can touch the client without physically touching him or her. This is still a delicate and perhaps a bit controversial topic. Some of our clients are people that have been sexually abused. They will not allow touching, at least not until they can trust the counselor or are healed. Other people, because of their cultural background don't believe in physical touch. The CAPE Approach itself is not a physically touching approach. This is left up to each individual counselor. The CAPE Approach will touch the soul of the individual. This is where it hurts and that is why they came for help.

Remember Ruth Ann, they young lady I told you about in my introduction? She would not allow anyone to physically touch her. If she saw someone getting close to her, she would shout, "Don't touch me, get away from me." As a matter of fact, she would yell that phrase in her sleep. Before going into my "selfish behavior", the "C" of the CAPE Approach had been put to action and a week later she was describing what compassion had done for her. She said she had never known what love was and now she was scared because she did not know how to handle it. She said it was like jumping up and down in a bed full of white chicken feathers. Even if she fell, she would not be hurt. After several weeks of compassionate and empathic caring, Ruth Ann had allowed one of us to touch her, to CAPE her.

What are some of the causes of emotional instability or crisis that would cause a person to be "CAPED"? In my opinion, all of the emotional problems a person experiences are derived from the following ten categories I refer to as Emotional Threatening Events (ETE):

1-Low self-esteem/Low self-image

2-Grief

3-Loneliness

4-Past and present victimization and abuse

5-Cultural shock

6-Life stresses related to work, school or family

7-Lack of communication

8-Spiritual instability

9-Satanic oppression/possession

10-Health and physical issues

As the counselor questions the client, she will be able to identify which ETE the client is experiencing. It will give her a picture of the client's belief system.

Following is a list of causes of ETE that can be used by individuals in the helping ministry or helping profession, especially those who are beginning their career in the field such as interns and counselor trainees or those who are compassionate listeners such as lay people and Help Hotline volunteers.

1. **Low self-esteem** stems from rejection, ridicule, neglect, and emotional abuse.

2. **Grief** is derived from, among other things, the loss of a job, a miscarriage, the loss of a loved one due to death, separation or divorce. Empty nests will be another cause of grief. As I write this book, I'm grieving over the loss of so many thousands of people during the terrorist attack that happened here in America and that I told you about in Chapter 2.

    There are thousands grieving their loved ones that either died, were hurt or lost their jobs because of this gruesome act. Others are grieving their second home, called the work place. Many New Yorkers are grieving the lost of the World Trade Towers that were destroyed by the blast. The people in Washington, DC are grieving the destruction of part of the Pentagon. The firefighters and police officers are grieving their comrades that died trying to safe others. We are all grieving simultaneously; but we are all grieving differently and for a different loss.

The counselor in a situation like this must be wise and understanding about the magnitude of this grief and not allow his or her own grief to interfere with the services he or she is to provide. This is where the counselor applies the CAPE Approach on his/herself as described in chapter 4.

3. **Loneliness** can be caused by rejection, abandonment, neglect, death, and separation from a loved one or lack of communication. Newness on a job or in a

community can also be the cause of loneliness. Divorce or separation can cause loneliness, too.

4. **Past and present victimization and abuse** are the result of physical or sexual abuse as a child or adult. Sexual abuse includes physical contact, any type of sexual penetration, forced or unforced, and oral sex. It also includes touching the victim's body with or without clothing and fondling his or her private parts. Victimization could have also occurred in a visual manner such as a father pretending he forgot something in the bathroom and walking in to get it while the daughter is naked taking a shower.

Emotional abuse can be cause in many ways. I'll only mention some examples for the benefit of Help Hotlines volunteers, lay people and non-professional caregivers. Various examples of emotional abuse are words that are demeaning, belittling, insulting to the hearer. This abuse can be directed by one spouse to the other, parents to their children, teachers to students, or caregivers to their clients. In reality, anybody can emotionally abuse another person, but emotional abuse has a more profound impact if the abuser is someone who has some sort of emotional tie to the abused.

5. **Cultural shock** can be caused by either moving from one country to another, one community to another, from one school to another, from one church to another, from one job to another or from one foster family to another.

6. **Life stressors** can come from work, school, the community, church, or family. People also can feel stressed out when they don't feel understood or appreciated. Stressors can hit us from all angles. Illnesses and deaths in the family or extended family is the cause of great stress. Good events can also bring stresses into peoples' lives. Examples are the birth of

child, the wedding of a loved one, the buying of a home, and even wining the "jackpot."

7. **Lack of communication**. Many times we speak but no one listens. They can hear but cannot listen. No compassion, no empathy. This can cause misunderstandings, family feuds, broken marriages, broken relationships, and rebellious teenagers. Lack of communication has been the cause of closing of some businesses.

I remember a friend I'll call Carmen. She went in business with a good friend of hers. The business was flourishing. The place looked marvelous. One day she told me that she was breaking up the partnership with her friend. As a matter of fact, they were not talking to each other! When I ask why the decision of breaking the business contract, she answered it was because of lack of communication. She said that her partner would make important business decisions without communicating them to her and that in other cases she would not follow through with what was expected of her but never communicated it to her partner. This lack of communication between these two friends was the cause of a business failure.

8. **Spiritual instability or lack of spirituality.** Some clients may complain that although they are believers they don't seem to grow spirituality. They've reached a plateau and no matter how hard they try, they can't mature spiritually. They remain babies in the Lord. Some causes of spiritual instability are problems of the past. Some times is due to external pressure from the body of Christ for individuals to grow without anyone digging down into the root of their problem. Sometimes, roots need to be cut or branches pruned

before the plant begins blooming. The same is true with spiritual growth.

Kelly, Jr. (1995) gives the following wise advise to counselors:

The counselor's knowledge of a client's conservative, fundamentalist, or liberal religious orientation, along with some understanding of the content of the client's spiritual and religious belief, provides an increasingly elaborate schema that the counselor may refine and use to understand each client's individual, idiosyncratic spiritual or religious attitudes as these are relevant to counseling (p. 29).

Lack of spirituality can have many roots; one root can be doubt about the doctrine. Another reason for lack of spirituality can be lack of trust in the leader or leaders, or lack of personal time alone meditating in God's Word. It is important that the counselor listen carefully in order to be able to help the client with his or her doubts.

9. **Satanic oppression/possession**. There is a difference between satanic oppression and satanic possession. Christians cannot be possessed. When a person is born again, the Holy Spirit of God moves in them. The Bible tells us that He that lives within us is greater than he of the world. The Bible also says in 1 John 4: 13, "By this we know that we abide in Him, and He in us, because He has given us of His Spirit." Good rules over evil, therefore, the belief that a born again Christian is possessed by Satan is not true. Satan wants us to believe that because it will leave an open door for doubt and Satanic oppression. Nevertheless, my standing is that Satan can possess a non-believer of God. A person

either serves God or Satan. We cannot serve both. One example of demonic possession is found in Mark 5:2-5, it reads:

An when He had come out of the boat, immediately there met Him out of the tombs a man with an unclean spirit, who had his dwelling among the tombs; and no one could bind him, not even with chains, because he had often been bound with shackles and chains. And the chains had been pulled apart by him, and the shackles broken in pieces; neither could anyone tame him. And always, night and day, he was in the mountains and in the tombs, crying out and cutting himself with stones.

This is one of the most dramatic examples of satanic possession found in the Bible. This case, along with the one found in Matthew 8:28-30, are examples of two severe cases of mental disorder. In today's society, these individuals would perhaps be locked up in a mental health hospital and heavily sedated. Yet we find these cases in the Bible as a consolation and example to the Christian counselor, pastor, and lay worker that all things are possible with God. They are vivid examples of how Jesus used the CAPE Approach to help people in crises.

10. **Health and physical issues**. Counselors and clinicians today meet with many patients who claim somatic disorders. Our present life style has a lot to do with this problem. People have neglected to remember that their bodies are temples of the Holy Spirit Who lives in them and Whom they received from God (1 Corinthians 6:

19). Some have bad eating habits, other have bad sleeping habits or bad working habits. All of these elements can contribute to health and physical issues. Other physical problems are due to untreated emotional problems such as depression.

By understanding the basis to a client's ETE and using the CAPE Approach to gain trust from the client; the counselor, pastor or layperson can rest assured that they are going in the right direction in helping the client. Christ whispers to the counselor, "You can do all things through Me that gives you strength" (Philippians 4:13). (Paraphrased by writer) He also assures the counselor that He has sent the Holy Spirit, who is going to be his Helper and his own Counselor.

Christ also tells those in the helping profession and ministry in Philippians 4:6, "Be anxious for nothing, but in everything by, prayer and supplication, with thanksgiving, let your requests be made known to God."

By using the CAPE Approach, the counselor will not need to be anxious, because she knows that through her compassion for the hurting client, her action in making her request known to God, by her prayer of supplication and thanksgiving, and her empathic attitude, all will be well with her client! Perhaps not immediately, perhaps not the way she would like, but all will be well in God's way and timing.

Judith A. Justiniano-Houts

Chapter 4

Rest For The Counselor

In order to remain effective in the helping profession, the counselor needs to reflect on his or her own feelings. He or she first needs to process any personal emotions interfering with the treatment of the client. Most times the best exercise to start out with is with the renewing of the mind. This exercise is very helpful and soothing when done in between sessions.

The Bible tells us in Ephesians 4:23, "...be renewed in the spirit of your mind."

It is very important that counselors take breaks between counseling sessions in order to renew their minds. A break will help to clear their minds of any prejudice, personal memories, frustrations, apathy or restlessness, and boredom that may have come upon them during their last counseling session.

The Apostle Paul exhorts the saints of God through the inspiration of the Holy Spirit to let go of "all bitterness, wrath, anger, clamor, and evil speaking... and be kind to one another, tenderhearted..." (Ephesians 4:31,32). If the counselor goes from one session to the next without taking shorts breaks in between, she is opening herself up to apathy, boredom, and bad judgment. Even Jesus took time to enter solitude (breaks) after ministering to the people. We find that after feeding the five thousand, Jesus told His disciples to get into the boat and go and wait for Him at the other side of the lake while He dismissed the multitude. Mathew 14:23 say, "And when he had sent the multitude away, He went up on a mountain by *Himself* (emphasis by writer) to pray."

Jesus saw the importance of the renewing of the mind through prayer and meditation. This is the example Jesus left for the Christian counselors today. Kottler (1993) also talks about the importance of counselors taking time for themselves to avoid burnout and stress. He says,

Some therapists are great advocates of work breaks used as buffers against stress, as emotional breathers providing time and space to unwind, and as safety valves to blow off stem (Maslach, 1986). For some practitioners this simply means not scheduling so many appointments consecutively. Other clinicians are more systematic in their efforts. As one person relates, "Since I normally start to drag in the early afternoon and begin asking myself why I am still doing this kind of work after all these years, I have learned to program the hours from 2:00 to 4:00 for my own mental health.

I read somewhere that this is the time when most mammals take naps and when most industrial accidents take place. I can believe it. Anyway, I take time out from my day to go for a walk, to work out, or to read a novel" (p. 174).

Christian counselors should take to heart Kottler's advice. It is during this time of solitude that the Christian counselor can apply the CAPE Approach to his or her own personal needs in order to renew their mind and soul; to recharge their spirit. It is a good way to remain in compassion through out the day. When the counselor has compassion for him or herself, then it becomes easier to have compassion for others. The Lord tells us to love our neighbor as we love ourselves.

<u>Using the CAPE Approach for Self-Therapy</u>

<u>A Godly Advice for the Counselor</u>

There are different approaches to self-therapy. The goal is for the counselor to keep his or her own sanity in order to provide the best service to the clients. I've read that some individuals recommend yoga, meditation and stress relieving exercises. Others recommend that we in the helping profession field get our own counselor or confidant. I'm not here to either recommend or criticize these methods. I want to give the counselors another alternative.

Kottler (1993) explains my point of a counselor taking care of him or herself better. He gives us examples of how it is done by some clinicians and past experts in the field. He says that some counselors keep journals. One of these journal keepers was Carl Jung, he explained. Kottler says,

"Carl Jung was the first to recognize the merits of the diary for a practicing therapist" (p. 226). "Others", Kottler says, "have a confidant, or a professional therapist as a confidant. Yet others like Freud wrote letters to colleagues" (p. 227). I am in turn recommending using the CAPE Approach as another method of self-help.

Using the CAPE Approach on oneself is a very interesting and holistic experience. We've heard about self-talk. This is the same technique except that the counselor is using the Christ-Like-Approach to enrich his or her own soul. This can be done either during short breaks taken throughout the day, or during the long break taken at the end of the day.

The CAPE Approach method will not take long but the counselor can stretch it as long as he or she wants, depending how stressed out or tired he or she feels.

I've practiced this approach on myself while driving to a stressful meeting. I've practiced it when frustrated because business or family affairs have not gone how I've wanted them to go. I've applied it before a prayer meeting or a public speaking engagement. I apply the technique before I meet with my clients and after they are gone. It is like diving into a pool of fresh cool and clear water after a hot sunny day or like splashing cold water in your face when you are studying for a final exam. It just gives one new energy and new insights. Following is the recommended way to do it:

Compassion. I must have compassion for myself by understanding my own feelings and emotions and separating them from the feelings of my clients. Christ lives in me; therefore, I can do all things through Christ that gives me the strength. I am a new creation, therefore, right this minute I am being refreshed and become a new person;

new ideas, new understanding, new focus. Compassion is love in action!

Action. I must take action to love myself, action to forgive myself and to accept forgiveness from others and from God. I will have agape love for myself, and for those around me. I will unselfishly love my clients regardless of how they look, how they like, act, or their belief system.

Prayer. I will pray for wisdom and for the regeneration of my own mind. I will pray for the cleansing of my soul and for the direction of the Holy Spirit as I minister to my client. This is a good time for the counselor to symbolically put on the "Armor of God" (Ephesians 6:11).

Another good prayer for the counselor to pray is found in James 1:5, "If any of you lacks wisdom, let him ask of God, who gives to all liberally and without reproach, and it will be given to him." Helping professionals are not born with Godly wisdom to deal with the kinds of problems the clients bring in with them. They must request it as James tells us. The promise is that He will give it *liberally*. It is very relaxing to know that as Christian counselors we don't have to depend on ourselves nor on our own wisdom, but on the wisdom of God. But we need to request it. These are several examples of prayers the counselor, pastor, or layperson can pray for himself, herself, or clients. There are many more prayers in the Bible to choose from, nevertheless, the best prayer, is the spoken one, coming out of a sincere and humble heart.

Empathy. The counselor can pray empathy into his or her heart while meditating on the following positive self-talk developed by yours truly. "I enthusiastically press on in the ministry of help and compassion. I enter into this ministry in the name of the Father, of the Son, and of the Holy Spirit. I pray that I will never practice apathy or sympathy, but that I will always practice empathy with my clients. I will take an empathic attitude and always have a listening ear. I empty myself of prejudice and false biases and accept the empathic mind of Christ. With the mind of Christ I will be able to do all things because He strengthens me."

Chapter 5

Stepping Out of Compassion

Should the Christian counselor constantly be compassionate? Let's look at Jesus' example. He is our role model. Jesus was not compassionate all the time. This was because not all situations called for compassion. We find this in Mark 11: 15-17

...Jesus entered the temple area and began driving out those who where buying and selling there. He overturned the tables of the money changers and the benches of those selling doves, and would not allow anyone to carry merchandise through the temple courts. And as he taught them he said, "Is it not written: "My house will be called a house of prayer for all nations'?

But you have made it 'a den of robbers.'"

As we can see, Jesus was angry. His actions, His words, and His tone of voice reflect this emotion. It was a rightful and holy anger. It is what psychologists and clinicians might call a healthy anger. It was His zeal for God's place and God's people that triggered the anger. Was He wrong for not being compassionate towards the perpetrators? No! If we read between the lines, we can see that He was being compassionate with those that had been robbed of the blessing of the Word, but had no compassion for those that did them wrong by being concerned about themselves and their own fleshly satisfaction (making money by selling animals for the sacrifice to those that didn't bring one.)

Therefore is a counselor unjust or unmerciful for not displaying compassion in some situations? No! The Bible tells us that God will have compassion on whomever He has compassion. This means that there are special situations when compassion is not going to do any good to the individual because that individual has made up his or her mind to do evil. Let's review Romans 9: 14-15. "What shall we say then? Is there unrighteousness with God? Certainly not! For He says to Moses, "I will have mercy on whomever I will have mercy, and I will have compassion on whomever I will have compassion."

The same thing is true with the Christian counselor. There are times when a client comes for counseling because it was either mandated by the court or the job. In her heart she has no desire to listen or to cooperate with the counselor. Sometimes this individual is ready to make war with the counselor. In these types of situations, I have heard that some counselors, after trying compassion with no result, have terminated the counseling sessions and stopped being compassionate. Did the counselor do wrong? No indeed!

On other occasions, the counselor takes steps to protect an innocent child who has been, or is being, sexually or physically abused by an adult. By reporting the abuse, he or she is showing compassion towards the child and no compassion to the perpetrator. There are times that the perpetrator is the client and confesses to the crime. It is in situations like this that the counselor has the right to step out of compassion for the client and report what he or she has learned in order to save an innocent victim. Is he or she being unjust and apathetic? The perpetrator might think so, but he or she is protecting the abused person.

Other reasons for the counselor, or any member of the helping profession, to step out of compassion is when he or she sees a colleague violating ethical issues, such as having sexual relations with a client, violating confidentiality issues or sees evidence of danger to the client. It is the responsibility of the compassionate counselor to be full of Godly anger and confront the colleague or report him or her to the superiors.

So, although he or she is not compassionate toward the client (the person violating the law), he or she is demonstrating compassion to those whose rights are being violated. The counselor is following Jesus' example. By confronting the individual engaged in the unethical action, and reporting abuse of children, the counselor is stepping out of compassion for one, but respecting the dignity and worth of the other. Van Hoose and Kottler (1987) talk about "respecting the dignity and worth of the individual and striving for the preservation and protection of fundamental human rights" (p. 171). This can be interpreted as stepping out of compassion when necessary.

As one can see, even when a counselor steps out of compassion, indirectly he or she is being compassionate to those who cannot defend themselves. So, in reality, a Christian counselor never loses the capacity to be compassionate, but will have no compassion on those who do evil.

At this point in America, because of the terrorist attack just days ago, the nation has no compassion for those terrorists who did this horrible act of violence. If for example, one of the terrorists came to your office to counsel or confess his crime, what would you do?

It is easy to let anger and hate rise up and take revenge. God says, "Beloved, do not avenge yourselves, but rather give place to wrath; for it is written, "Vengeance is Mine, I will repay" (Romans 12:19). I believe that although we will have no compassion for the individual as a person for what he has done, we should have compassion for his soul.

It is from this frame of mind then that the counselor needs to work. Confession of sin and restitution of that which was destroyed is one of the first things that must be explained to this client and then the asking and receiving of God's forgiveness for the atrocity. In cases like this it is the soul we worry about and let the authorities handle the rest.

Judith A. Justiniano-Houts

Chapter 6

Conclusion

When one talks about a thunderstorm, the first thing that comes to our mind is the pouring down of rain accompanied by lightning, high winds, hail, and of course, very cloudy skies. We've all seen, heard or watched a movie with scenes as described above.

The first instinct of a person caught in a thunderstorm is to look for shelter. If we are already sheltered and happen to see a person out in the storm our instinct then is to get them to a safe place where they are warm and dry.

I've never been able to forget a certain snowstorm. I was twelve years old and lived in Hoboken, NJ. This was a church night. A girlfriend and I decided to go to church in spite of the bad weather. Our parents made no effort to stop us. We put our winter boots on, our heavy coat, and wool gloves and took off. We happily and giggly walked the 12 blocks to the church. When church was over, the storm had gotten worse. We had forgotten to ask our parents for bus money and those that had cars in the church had already left. We had no choice but to walk back home. Twelve blocks under blizzard conditions for two young girls felt like an eternity. Our ears were frozen, our feet were heavy, our fingers felt like ice and it was very, very hard to continue walking.

Finally we made it home, and when we entered the building, the only thing we could do was yell for help. I remember my parents running down the stairs of a five-story building. My father and mother picked us up; they carried us upstairs, wrapped us in warm blankets and prepared hot chocolate for us to drink. They brought to us warm water and put our feet and hands in it. Oh, how good it felt! The fear was gone, the pain dissipated and the comfort of loving parents assured us safety.

As we can see, the two key factors people in crisis are looking for are "warmth and safety." Jesus provides that for all of those who are in any type of emotional crisis. David says in Psalm 91: 2, "I will say of the LORD, "He is my refuge and my fortress; My God, in Him I will trust."

The CAPE Approach is to men and women in emotional crisis what the warm blanket was for me when my feet, fingers, ears, and nose where frozen. The CAPE Approach should be an extension of our fortress, God our Father. It symbolizes warmth, safety and comfort.

Christ should always be presented to those in emotional need as the only fortress, the unshakable shelter. The CAPE Approach is only a path to help direct the clients to the Fortress.

May God help you as you wander into the storms of life willing to help those who are hurting, confused, wounded and in the process of giving up hope. Christ is our hope. I see the CAPE Approach as a tool pointing the hurting ones to Christ our healer and our provider. I also see it as not only a warm blanket, but a fortress for the counselor who is so unselfishly helping God's children. More importantly, the CAPE Approach will keep both, counselor and client, safe under the shadow of the Almighty. The CAPE Approach will help keep the counselor alert, willing, compassionate and empathic towards the client. Remember that compassion is love in action, the action to pray and to be empathic with your client.

References

Adams, J. E. (1970). <u>Competent to Counsel</u>. Grand Rapids, MI: Zondervan Publishing House.

Allender, D. (1995). <u>Broken Trust</u>. (Video). Chicago, IL: Christian Counseling Resources, Inc.

Benner, D. (1992). Strategic Pastoral Counseling. Grand Rapids, MI: Baker Books.

Bradshaw, J. (1993). <u>Healing the Shame that Binds You.</u> Deerfield Beach, FL: Health Communications, Inc.

Collins, G. R., General Editor, (1991). <u>Excellence and Ethics in Counseling.</u> United States of America: Word Inc.

Justiniano-Houts, J. A. (1999). <u>A Call to Listen.</u> Unpublished manuscript.

Kiersey D. & Bates M. (1984). <u>Please Understand Me.</u> Del Mar, CA: Prometheus Nemesis Book Company.

Kelly, E. W., Jr. (1995). <u>Spirituality and Religion in Counseling and Psychotherapy.</u> Alexandria, VA: American Counseling Association.

Kottler, J. A. (1993). <u>On Being a Therapist.</u> (Rev. ed). San Francisco, CA: Jossey-Bass Publishers.

Slaikeu, K. A. (1984). <u>Crisis Intervention</u> (2nd ed). Needham Heights, MA: Allyn and Bacon.

Van Hoose W. & Kottler, J. A. (1987). <u>Ethical and Legal Issues in Counseling and Psychotherapy</u> (2nd ed). San Francisco, CA: Jossey-Bass Publishers.

About the Author

Dr. Judith A. Justiniano-Houts is the founder and Executive Director of the Agape Ministry-Crisis Prevention and Intervention Center in Pataskala, Ohio. She was also the founder and Executive Director of the Agape Haus, Inc. in Battle Creek, Michigan, a human services agency providing services to people who fell through the gaps of the Welfare System, which included support groups for abused women. She founded and directed, for ten years, the award-winning Christian Hotline, called the Agape LifeLine. Before being ordained as a minister, Justiniano-Houts was a missionary to Columbia, South America, where she ministered to many in need, not only spiritual need but physical, spiritual, and emotional. She has started two bilingual churches, one in Michigan, and the other in Ohio. She is a mediator, a coach, and a mentor. Justiniano-Houts has mentored many young men and women in not only becoming a better citizen by staying in school, but also becoming a better Christian. She is an instructor and develops custom-made training for the needs of the churches or agencies. Dr. Houts is a seminar presenter and a public speaker with speaking engagements ranging from civic organizations to Federal agencies. Justiniano-Houts had her own local television and radio program in Battle Creek, Michigan. Actually, she not only pastors the Agape Ministry Church, but she also counsels women who are survivors of sexual and emotional abuse, and mediates and counsels couples.

She received her B.A. from Nazareth College in Michigan and her Ph.D. from LaSalle University in Mandeville, Louisiana. She received her Marriage Works Certificate from the American Association for Christian Counselors, and a Leadership Certificate from the Battle Creek Leadership Academy. Presently, she is working towards her Master's Degree in Community Counseling through the University of Dayton, Ohio.